Jimmy Jonny Brownie Stays Up All Night

by Bing Puddlepot

For Mom, Tracy and Ellen

Library of Congress Cataloging-in-Publication Data

Puddlepot, Bing, 1967-
Jimmy Jonny Brownie stays up all night / by Bing Puddlepot ; illustrated by Sherwin G. Schwartzrock.
p. cm.
Summary: Jimmy Jonny Brownie always tries to delay bedtime as long as
possible--until he learns what happens when he stays up all night one night.
ISBN 0-9676148-1-3
[1. Bedtime--Fiction. 2. Sleep--Fiction.] I. Schwartzrock, Sherwin G., 1970- ill. II. Title.
PZ7.P94969 Ji 2000   [E]--dc21   99-088135

Jimmy Jonny Brownie had trouble going to bed.
In fact, he did everything he could to stay up.

He put his jammies
on backwards.

He gobbed too much toothpaste
on his toothbrush.

He got his hands stuck
in his mouth while he flossed.

His mom and dad, of course, didn't let bed time get
too late. His backwards pajamas were left backwards.
They had him brush with all the toothpaste he squirted
out, so as not to waste any. They even read to him
with his hands jammed into his mouth. (As everyone
knows, hands are very tough things to get stuck in mouths,
and very easy things to get out.)

One morning, when everyone was saggy-eyed
from trying to get Jimmy Jonny Brownie to bed
the night before, Jimmy Jonny asked...

..."Dad, can I stay up all night?"

His dad thought about it.

Rubbed his chin, smiled, and said,

"I think *that* is a splendid idea."

Had he heard right? Up all night?! His dad nodded.
This was the day—or night, as the case may be—Jimmy Jonny
had been waiting for his whole life.

As time came for Jimmy Jonny to get ready for bed, no one
mentioned hopping in the bath, or putting on pajamas,
or brushing teeth, or getting two books, or singing a goodnight song,
or saying prayers, or tucking in the covers tight,
or getting a kiss goodnight.

They just sat there. Mom read the newspaper. Dad read a book.
So Jimmy Jonny grabbed a big stack of his own books, sat beside
them on the couch and looked at the pictures.

A clock ticked in the background.

Many ticks later, Jimmy Jonny's mom stretched and said, "I'm heading for bed." Dad said, "Me, too."

Jimmy Jonny Brownie just smiled
and said, "Good night everyone," and headed happily
off to his room to stay up some more.
He looked at the clock; it said ten, which was two
hours past his bedtime!

Pushing back the
curtains, he smiled
at the dark sky,
shining with stars.

He taped a piece of paper over his flashlight, poked holes with a pencil and made his own stars on the ceiling. Holding the flashlight between his feet, he launched his rocket upwards. It banged off the ceiling, clunked him on the noggin, bounced against the dresser and rolled under the bed.

Which is where he found his yo-yo! Sending the yo-yo down was fine, but he was a size short to bring it back up.

Hunting for something to stand on, Jimmy Jonny found the box of dominoes.

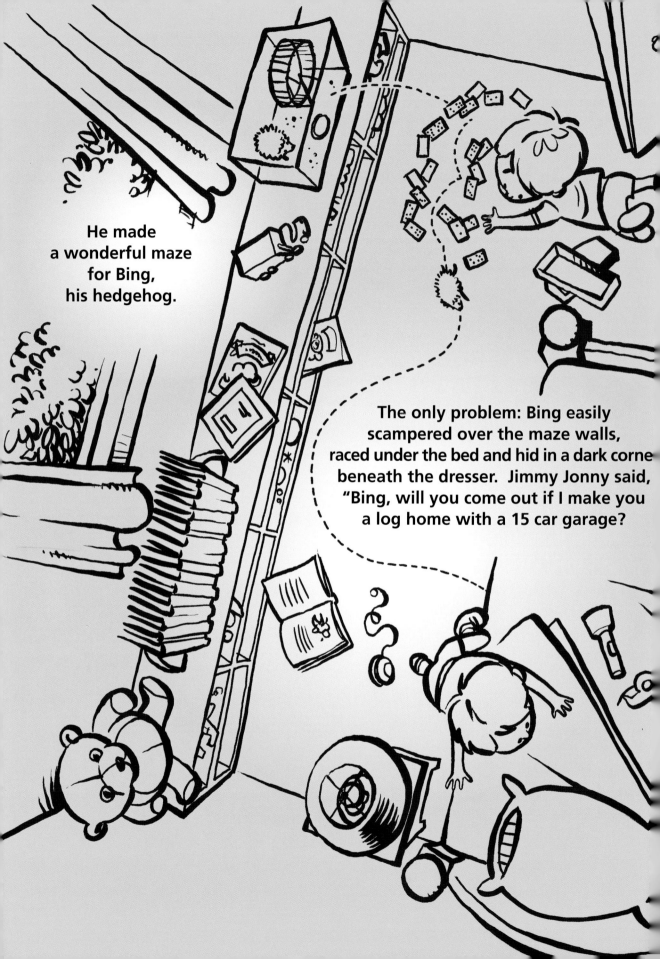

He made
a wonderful maze
for Bing,
his hedgehog.

The only problem: Bing easily
scampered over the maze walls,
raced under the bed and hid in a dark corne
beneath the dresser. Jimmy Jonny said,
"Bing, will you come out if I make you
a log home with a 15 car garage?

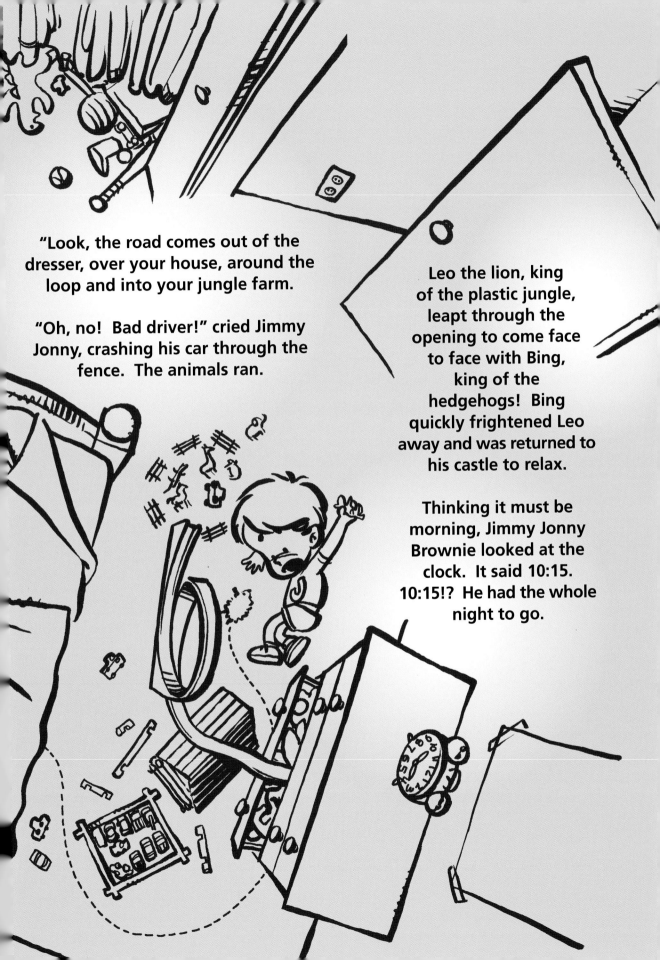

"Look, the road comes out of the dresser, over your house, around the loop and into your jungle farm.

"Oh, no! Bad driver!" cried Jimmy Jonny, crashing his car through the fence. The animals ran.

Leo the lion, king of the plastic jungle, leapt through the opening to come face to face with Bing, king of the hedgehogs! Bing quickly frightened Leo away and was returned to his castle to relax.

Thinking it must be morning, Jimmy Jonny Brownie looked at the clock. It said 10:15. 10:15!? He had the whole night to go.

Trotting off to the bathroom, he sampled water from several paper cups. He stacked the cups into a wall. He knocked them down. He lined them up. A cup parade! He brought a cup back for Bing to try. Bing wasn't interested.

Jimmy Jonny Brownie then watched the shadows
on the wall. At first they scared him. But he couldn't stay up all night
if he was afraid of shadows, he told himself. So he made some nice
shadows of his own. They asked him if he liked to camp.

Off his bed came the covers and sheets for the tent. Off came
the pillow and mattress. He built a flashlight campfire. He fished
off the dock.   He relaxed on the shore trying to learn how to whistle.

Had he nodded off?

Looking up, Jimmy Jonny saw sunlight creeping
into his room and heard his parents' alarm clock. He had done it!
Jimmy Jonny Brownie had stayed up all night! Hearing
stumbly footsteps in the hall, Jimmy Jonny opened his door,
and yelled at his stunned dad, "I stayed up all night!"

"Great," his dad mumbled tiredly. "Don't forget that Ellie Knelly is coming over to play today. We'll have to make sure your room is cleaned after breakfast."

That was the last thing Jimmy Jonny Brownie remembered very clearly. At breakfast, he fell asleep with his chin in his glass of orange juice. After breakfast, Jimmy Jonny fell asleep as he cleaned his room.

The dominoes gave him polka dots all over his face, Ellie noticed as she woke him up. Being the thoughtful girl she was, she helped him clean while giggling quietly to herself.

At which point he fell asleep on the floor. Ellie soon got bored
with coloring Jimmy Jonny's coloring books...

...and started coloring Jimmy Jonny.

Which lasted until his mom called them for lunch.
His favorite: spaghetti.

Ellie apologized to Jimmy Jonny
for coloring him and felt bad.
He said a sleepy, "It's okay," before
he laid his head down in the
spaghetti. "I think we need to get
out the swimming pool for you
guys," his mom said to Ellie.
Ellie smiled.

Ellie Knelly and Jimmy Jonny always have terrific water fun in the pool. That is, except when Jimmy Jonny falls backwards out of the pool, fast asleep. Ellie found that water wakes people up very fast.

Jimmy Jonny Brownie
stayed awake until he fell asleep
again sliding down the slide.

And swinging.

And while counting against a tree
while Ellie went to hide.
Ellie wondered why no one came
to find her, until she spied Jimmy
Jonny Brownie fast asleep.

Ellie called her dad
to take her home.

Jimmy Jonny
Brownie didn't
wake up for setting
the table,
or eating dinner,
or washing dishes,
or taking a bath,
or putting on pajamas,
or brushing teeth,
or getting two books,
or singing a
goodnight song,
or saying prayers,
or tucking
in the covers tight
or getting a kiss
goodnight.

He just slept.

After that night, Jimmy Jonny decided that maybe
going to bed wasn't such a hard thing after all. He crawled in
all by himself, which made his parents very proud.

And it gave Jimmy Jonny Brownie
a whole lot of energy the next day.